Spring Is Here!

A Story About Seeds

By Joan Holub

Illustrated by Will Terry

SCHOLASTIC INC.

New York Toronto London Auckland Sydney
Mexico City New Delhi Hong Kong Buenos Aires

For Sheri Leider,
with thanks –J. H.

For Jocelyn –W. T.

ISBN-13: 978-0-545-15371-3
ISBN-10: 0-545-15371-9

18 17 16 15 14 13   16 17 18/0

Printed in the U.S.A.   40

First Scholastic printing, March 2009

Designed by Lisa Vega
The text of this book was set in font Century Oldstyle BT.

"A seed," says Reed.

"Lots more!"
says Tor.

"Plant them," says Em.

"Add dirt," says Curt.

"Now grow!" says Joe.

"Just wait," says Kate.

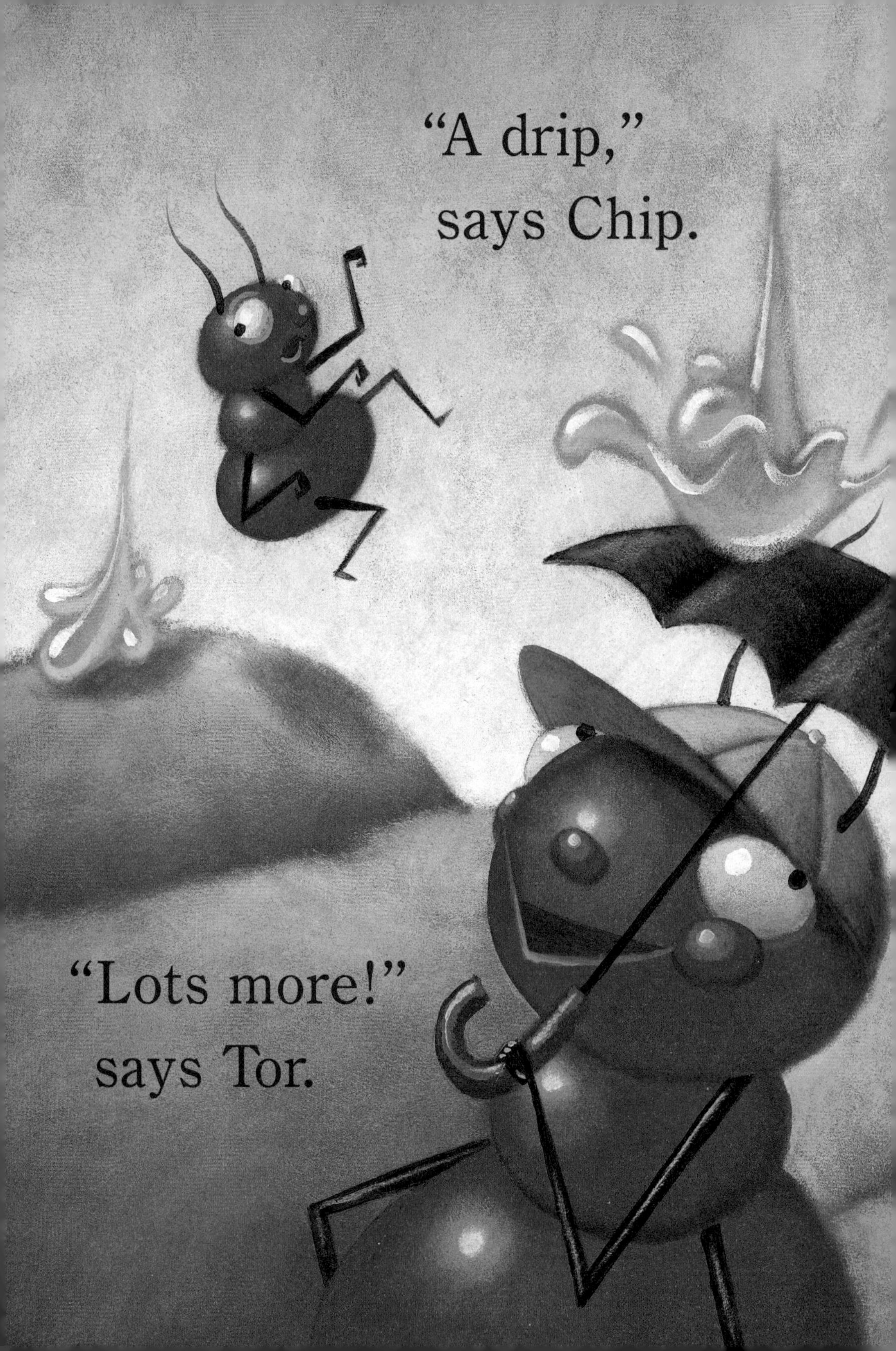

"A drip,"
says Chip.

"Lots more!"
says Tor.

"Yay! Rain!"
says Jane.

"Splish, splash,"
goes Nash.

"Splash, splish,"
goes Trish.

"A lake!" says Jake.

"Dive in,"
says Lynn.

"A raft," says Taft.

"Hop on,"
says Dawn.

"Blue sky,"
says Guy.

"Rainbow!" yells Joe.

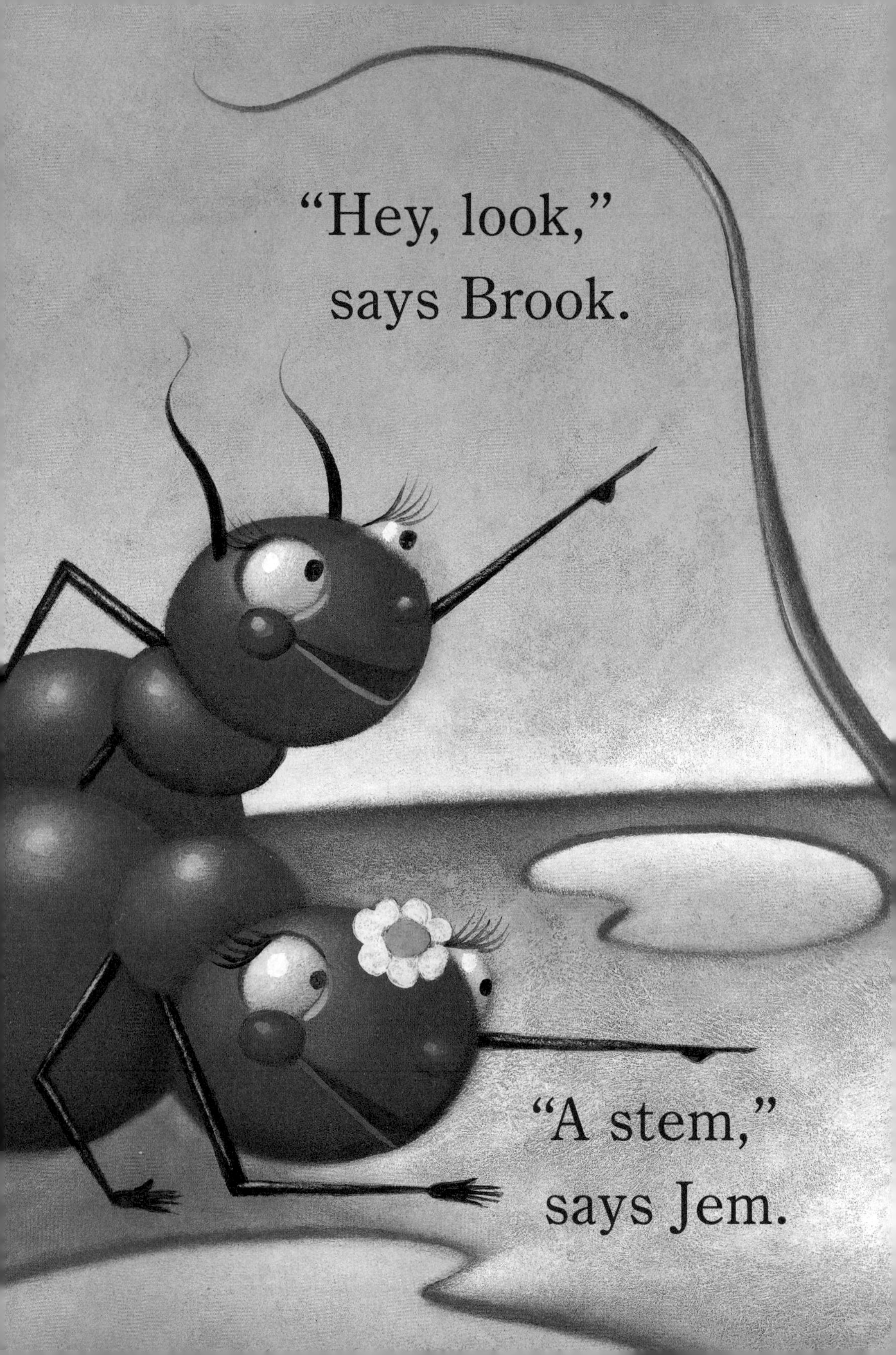

"Hey, look,"
says Brook.

"A stem,"
says Jem.

"And leaves,"
says Reeves.

"A bud," says Judd.

"Blooms, too,"
says Drew.

"Lots more!"
says Tor.

"Spring is here!"

The ants cheer.

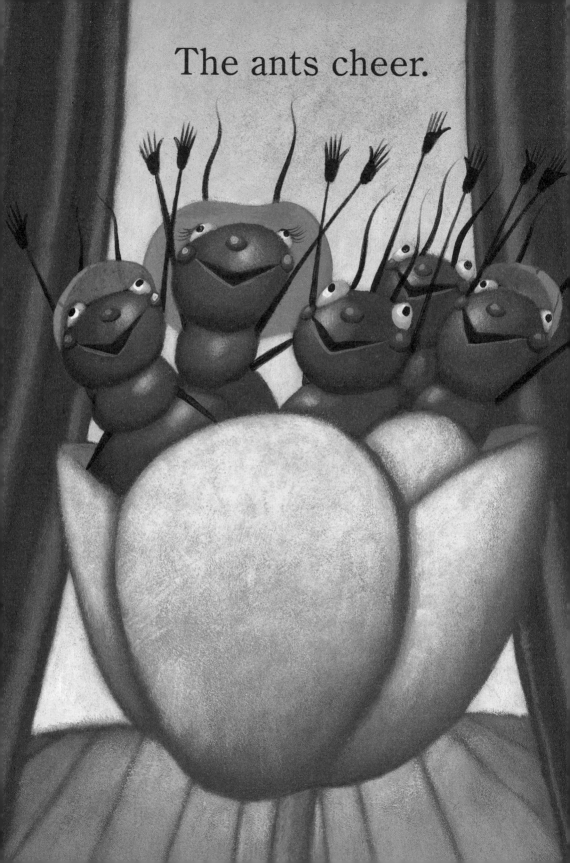